There go a Bug, a Boy,
and a Bear.

The Bear digs the dirt.

The Bug plants seeds.
The Boy waters them.

The seeds grow into plants.
A rabbit comes and eats them.

The Bear chases the rabbit
away—

but the rabbit comes back.

The Bug and the Bear
and the Boy build a fence.

Now the plants can grow.
And the rabbit can only watch.